THE YUCKIEST, STINKIEST, BEST VALENTINE EVER

THE YUCKIEST, STINKIEST, BEST VALENTINE EVER

BY BRENDA A. FERBER

PICTURES BY TEDD ARNOLD

PUFFIN BOOKS

FOR JACOB AND SAMMY, WHO ARE NEITHER YUCKY NOR STINKY.
I LOVE YOU BOTH! XOXO MOM
—B.A.F.

FOR OWEN, WITH HEARTS

—T.A.

PUFFIN BOOKS
An imprint of Penguin Random House LLC
375 Hudson Street
New York, New York 10014

First published in the United States of America by Dial Books for Young Readers,
a division of Penguin Young Readers Group, 2012
Published by Puffin Books, an imprint of Penguin Random House LLC, 2015

THE LIBRARY OF CONGRESS HAS CATALOGED THE DIAL BOOKS EDITION AS FOLLOWS:
Ferber, Brenda A.
The yuckiest, stinkiest, best valentine ever / by Brenda A. Ferber ; pictures by Tedd Arnold.
p. cm.
Summary: A young boy named Leon pursues a runaway valentine meant for his true love, Zoey Maloney.
ISBN 978-0-8037-3505-7 (hardcover)
[1. Valentine's Day—Fiction. 2. Love—Fiction.] 1. Arnold, Tedd, ill. II. Title.
PZ7.F3543Yu 2012
[e]—dc23
2011047668

Puffin Books ISBN 978-0-14-751709-8

Manufactured in China

1 3 5 7 9 10 8 6 4 2

LEON CUT A BIG
RED HEART OUT
OF CONSTRUCTION
PAPER. HE ADDED
ARMS, LEGS, AND
A FACE. WHAT A
SWEET VALENTINE!
HE TURNED IT
OVER AND WROTE:

Dear Zoey
Maloney,
I love you!

 Love,
Leon

BUT I THOUGHT VALENTINE'S DAY WAS ALL ABOUT **LOVE**.
HA! VALENTINE'S DAY IS ALL ABOUT CANDY. I'M TALKIN' CANDY HEARTS, CHOCOLATES, CARAMELS, **THE WORKS!**
HONEY B
SWEET HEART
B MINE

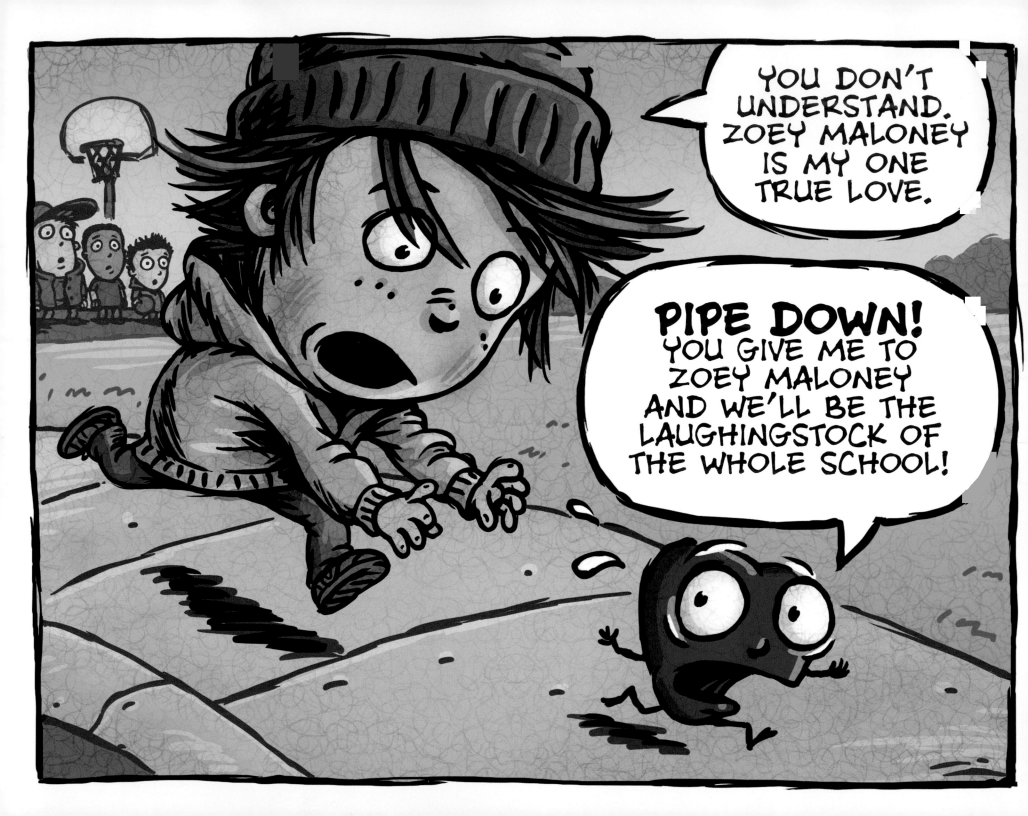

AND ON HE RAN, CALLING—
LOVE IS YUCKY. STINKY TOO. IT WILL TURN YOUR BRAIN TO GOO!

THEY CAME TO A FIELD WHERE SOME GIRLS WERE PLAYING TAG.

HELP! LEON THINKS HE'S IN LOVE WITH ZOEY MALONEY!

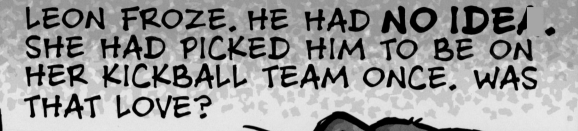

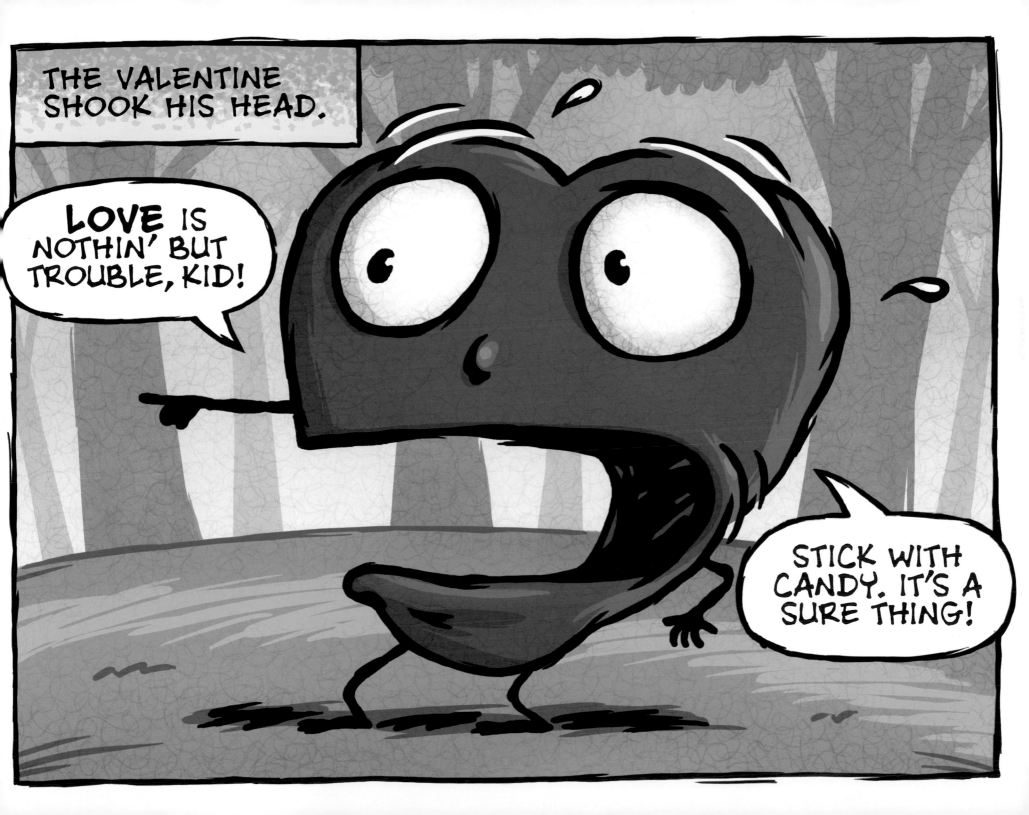

INTO TOWN RAN THE VALENTINE. AFTER HIM RAN LEON, THE BOYS, AND THE GIRLS, WHO WERE HOPING TO SEE **TRUE LOVE** TRIUMPH.

THE VALENTINE DASHED INSIDE SUGARMAN'S CANDY SHOP...

...WHERE HE SLAMMED INTO A GIRL WITH HAIR SLEEK AS SUNSHINE, EYES BRIGHT AS THE OCEAN, AND FRECKLES LIKE PERFECT SPECKS OF SAND...

A SMILE SPREAD ACROSS ZOEY MALONEY'S FACE. LEON'S HEART SOARED.

JUST THEN, THE VALENTINE NOTICED ZOEY MALONEY'S VALENTINE.

SWEET!

ZOEY MALONEY'S VALENTINE GIGGLED.

THE BOYS SAID—

WHOA!

THE GIRLS SAID—

OHH!

THE TEENAGERS SAID—

WAY TO GO!

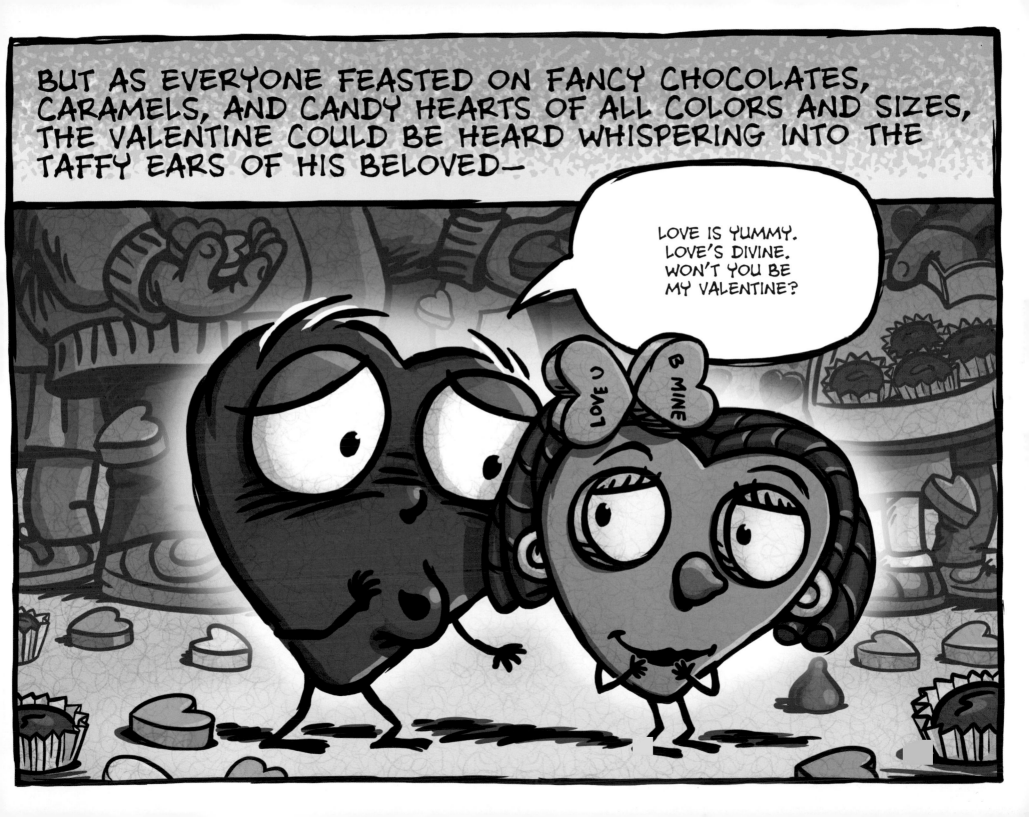